Henry at Home

Henry
at
Home

by Megan Maynor ✿ Illustrated by Alea Marley

Clarion Books | Houghton Mifflin Harcourt | Boston   New York

Clarion Books

3 Park Avenue,
New York, New York 10016

Text copyright © 2021 by Megan Maynor
Illustrations copyright © 2021 by Alea Marley

Clarion Books is an imprint of Houghton Mifflin Harcourt
Publishing Company.

hmhbooks.com

The illustrations in this book were done using Procreate and
finished in Photoshop.
The text was set in Andrade Pro and PlainPensle.
Cover design by Sharismar Rodriguez and Celeste Knudsen
Interior design by Sharismar Rodriguez and Celeste Knudsen

Library of Congress Cataloging-in-Publication Data is available.
ISBN 978-1-328-91675-4

Manufactured in China
SCP 10 9 8 7 6 5 4 3 2 1
4500820710

For Chloe and Emmett and Willa
–*M.M.*

For my sister, Gaby
–*A.M.*

As long as there had been Henry
and Liza, they were together.
   Liza and Henry.
   Henry and Liza.

"Henry, come see this!"

"Liza, look what I found!"

They knew all the same people.

And went to all the same parties.

They got haircuts at the same time.

Winter boots on the same day.

And flu shots together.

Sniff.
Sniff.

Liza never rescued
animals without Henry.
"Henry! A cheetah needs
our help!"

Henry never destroyed asteroids without Liza.
"Liza! Shields up! Blasters on!"

And their Best Place, the Twisty Tree,
was only for
Liza and Henry.
Henry and Liza.

One day, Liza got a backpack.

"Where's mine?" asked Henry.

"This is for school," said Liza.

"I want to go to school too,"
said Henry.

"You're not old enough yet,"
said Liza.

Liza also got a whole box of
pencils, fresh crayons, and her
own scissors.

"But I can write my name,"
said Henry. "And draw really
good birds. And I can use
scissors with no help."

"You'll go to school
next year," said Liza.

"Next YEAR?!" yelled Henry.
"Liza, you are so mean!"

"Henry, it's the rules."

Henry stomped on the crayons.

"HENRY!"

On the first day of school, Liza and her backpack climbed the big steps.

Without Henry.

The bus roared away.
And Henry roared too.

"ROARRRRRR!"

Henry stormed through the house.
He grabbed ALL the blankets
and ALL the pillows.

He built the biggest fort ever.
"No kindergartners allowed!" he yelled.

Henry burst out of the fort and announced,
"I can rescue animals WITHOUT Liza!"

He rescued so
many animals,
he needed a drink
of water.

"Also! I can blast asteroids without Liza!
Bew! Bew! Bew!"

"Haha! Best. Mission. Ever."

Henry circled the Twisty Tree,
but without Liza it seemed like a
Regular Place. So he zoomed on . . .

. . . to the swings.

It was tricky to get going without a
starter push from Liza.

But he did it.

Henry swung back and forth and
back and forth.

He swung so high, he touched
a leaf with his foot.

He swung so long,
he invented three new
swing tricks:

The Twister.

The Tall Guy.

And the most daring of them all,
the Falcon.

The bus roared by again.

"Henry! Guess what? I was the line leader. And I have
a new friend. And we have a class cheer!"

"Oh yeah? Well, I rescued animals. And I blasted asteroids.
And I invented three new swing tricks."

Henry swooshed toward the ground, arms
spread wide.

"Ah!" Liza covered her eyes.

Henry laughed. "That's called the Falcon."

Liza dropped her backpack. "Can I try?"

"I guess I could teach you," said Henry.

"How's your class cheer go?"

"I guess I could teach you," said Liza.

Hey, hey, what do you say?
We are ready for the day!

Hey, hey, what do you know?
We are here to learn and grow!

Liza and Henry swung and cheered.

After that Liza and Henry were not always together.

Sometimes Henry was sad to see Liza go.

Sometimes he was happy for her to leave.

They met new people.

And went to different parties.

But the Twisty Tree remained their
Best Place, always and forever only for
Liza and Henry.
Henry and Liza.